COME BACK!

JUDI FRIEDMAN

**Illustrated with photographs by
Stephen W. Kress and Others**

**Foreword by
Dr. Stephen W. Kress**

DODD, MEAD & COMPANY New York

PHOTOGRAPH CREDITS

Michael Hopiak, 77; Stephen W. Kress, 2-3, 14, 16-17, 18-19, 21, 22, 24, 26-27, 31, 34-35, 38, 39, 42, 46, 47, 48, 50, 51, 55, 57, 58-59, 62, 65, 69 (bottom), 73, 74, 80-81, 82, 83, 84, 85, 88-89, 91; and Duryea Morton, 53, 66-67, 69 (top), 70.

1   2   3   4   5   6   7   8   9   10

Library of Congress Cataloging in Publication Data

Friedman, Judi, date—
Puffins, come back!

Includes index.
SUMMARY: Discusses the Atlantic puffin, a hardy
colorful bird found in Greenland, Canada, Iceland, and
on islands near Scotland. Also describes a special
project sponsored by the National Audubon Society to
reestablish these birds in Maine.
1. Puffins—Juvenile literature.   [1. Puffins]
I. Kress, Stephen W.   II. Title.
QL696.C42F74   598′.33   80-2786
ISBN 0-396-07940-7

PUFFINS,
COME BACK!

PUFFINS,

To the men of my life:
  To my Father
    from whom I learned to love birds,
  To my Husband
    who gave me the courage to write about them,
  To my Son
    who understands. . . .

CONTENTS

Foreword by Dr. Stephen W. Kress   9

1. Alone on the Winter Ocean   13

2. A Special Bird   20

3. Dangers in the Past   29

4. Natural Dangers   33

5. Dangers from Humans   37

6. Saving the Puffin   41

7. Beginning the Experiment   45

8. Growing Up on Eastern Egg Rock   49

9. Preparing the Nesting Site   52

10. Raising Young Puffins   56

11. Chick Personalities   61

12. The Work of a Researcher   64

13. The Fledgling   72

14. Come Back, Little Brother   76

15. *Fratercula arctica*   79

16. An Unknown Future   87

     Index   93

FOREWORD

It was an overcast July day in 1970 when I first tried to land on Eastern Egg Rock. The Audubon boat named *Puffin III* tugged at its anchor, while our boatman rowed me in to examine the landing place. Harbor seals bobbed around us and then slipped back into the gray sea. But there were great foaming swells rolling onto the island that day—powerful waves that smashed against the rugged shores. My first landing would have to wait for another day. Yet this first encounter left a strong impression and, as I came to know the island better, an unusual vision haunted me.

Early Maine naturalists reported that Eastern Egg Rock once supported a thriving colony of Atlantic puffins. These most appealing birds nested under the island's great boulders, but sadly, hunters shot the birds for food and feathers, eliminating them from the island by 1880. One hundred years of absence, yet I could still imagine them winging in off the sea, delivering fish to their young.

Now, ten years after my first visit to Egg Rock, puffins are once again coming home to this tiny ocean island. The story of how our dedicated team achieved this remarkable end is capably told by Judi Friedman, who details the life history of the puffin and then explains how we used this knowledge to design a recovery plan.

Restoring puffins and other wildlife to former breeding range must be only part of long term plans to help rare and endangered wildlife. Puffins, for example, need more than safe breeding places, they must also have seas that are clean of poisons such as oil and pesticides, and waters that are abundant with fish. To slow the frightening loss of wild species, dedicated and responsible people will need to make careful studies and then develop sound management plans.

Efforts such as Project Puffin are important because they demonstrate the positive effects humans can have on their environment. All wild creatures deserve a place on earth, and it is the responsibility of each human generation to insist that no species should become extinct.

Stephen W. Kress
Ithaca, New York

PUFFINS,
COME BACK!

1. ALONE ON THE WINTER OCEAN

The North Atlantic Ocean can be a violent place. Wind storms can split ships' masts. Thirty-foot waves sometimes smash hulls. Tidal currents move motorless boats around like small toys. During winter storms, which can last for days, daylight and nighttime seem almost the same. Few sounds can be heard above the screaming wind and the crashing waves. Yet there is a small bird that spends much of its time all winter on the North Atlantic.

This bird is called the Atlantic puffin, and it is well equipped to survive this harsh environment. A thick layer of fat insulates its body against the icy cold water. Its feathers are waterproofed with its own special oil. Webbed feet help to propel it efficiently across the surface of the ocean. Short, but strong, wings act as underwater paddles. During fifty-mile-per-hour gale winds the puffin sometimes survives by

Puffins have wings long enough to permit flight in the air and just the right shape to propel them underwater.

diving beneath the powerful waves. It is also a good flier, although its wings are short. The puffin sometimes drops down in huge storm waves, then bounces up again, whirring over the ocean like a black-and-white skipping stone.

Even the eyes of the puffin help it to survive. All birds have an "extra" eyelid, but the eyelid of the puffin works under

14

the water. It acts like a little window, permitting clear vision under the surface.

For eight months, never touching land, Atlantic puffins swim in and fly over the ocean, covering hundreds of miles of rough and lonely sea. They even sleep on the water, their heads resting on their backs and tucked under their wings. During this period puffins usually stay in small groups.

Then spring comes. Something wonderful happens. From many parts of the North Atlantic Ocean puffins begin to swim and fly to the islands where they grew up. No one is sure how these birds are able to find their homes again. Perhaps they navigate by the stars, the location of the sun, tidal currents, or sense changes in the earth's magnetic field. Probably they use some combination of these skills because they can find their way under all weather conditions. It matters little if the sky is cloudy or if it is the foggiest day of spring—the puffins can find their way home.

For most of the 320,000 breeding pairs that still nest in North America, home is one of three islands located off the coast of Newfoundland. Great Island, the most important colony, is only one mile long and contains a colony of about 150,000 pairs—"wall-to-wall" birds!

Only one colony of Atlantic puffins still survives in the United States. It is located on Matinicus Rock off the coast of Maine. About one hundred pairs of puffins breed there.

By mid-April small groups of puffins are flying near

Puffin numbers at Great Island, Newfoundland. Here about 148,000 pairs of puffins nest, making it the largest colony in North America.

Matinicus Rock or swimming offshore. Then more of these birds appear, swimming together in great floating "rafts" of black-and-white bodies.

On arrival, hundreds of puffins may float offshore; the next day they may disappear back to the open sea. They return again and after a waiting period of several days—a time of inspection and communication—they circle and land near the familiar rocks and plants of their birthplace.

The older breeding birds are the first to stay. They land, explore and clean their burrows, pecking and pushing each

Male and female puffins. Colors are identical, but males usually are larger and have larger beak and head. Male (right), female (left).

other on the rocky cliffs. The breeding season has begun. This is the time when most people see puffins.

This book is solely about the Atlantic (or common) puffin. Atlantic puffins are found in Greenland, Canada, Iceland, and on islands near Scotland. Other species of puffins, which live in other areas, are the tufted and the horned puffins.

2. A SPECIAL BIRD

There is something very appealing about a puffin. Perhaps it is its sad look. Little, dark blue, horny plates run above the eyes, giving the puffin a rather worried appearance. Faint dark lines of feathers also run back from the eyes, looking a little like tearstains.

The cheeks of the puffin are fat, white, and "puffy." The bird looks like a small black-and-white penguin. Puffins stand upright—almost like little soldiers—in short uneven rows. Some people think that the puffin looks like a parrot and acts like a clown. It waddles when it walks and seems to almost bounce as it jumps from rock to rock. Sometimes a puffin will come back from a fishing trip loaded with twenty little fish hanging from its beak, giving the impression of a beard. People may laugh at the puffin's appearance, but they must marvel at how it keeps catching more fish while already holding ten or fifteen!

Three puffins pause momentarily with beaks loaded with tiny her-ring intended for their chicks which wait in rock crevice burrows.

Puffin face, side view. The bill develops bright colors as adaptations for courtship.

The adult puffin is a colorful bird. During the breeding season horny plates of red, blue-gray, and ivory run the length of the large triangular bill on both the male and the female. Little orange flower-like folds of skin brighten the corners of the beak. A bright red ring circles each eye. Legs and big webbed feet are bright red-orange. During the spring and summer puffins look like clowns dressed in fancy tuxedos.

The puffin is not aggressive unless cornered. Male birds

sometimes fight with their bills during the mating season. Few feathers fly, although the sharp beak can draw blood. Fights between these birds are often interrupted by nosy puffin neighbors. They crowd closely around. Their presence often stops the battle.

Although puffins push and peck each other, they seldom attack other birds. Rather, they are attacked—especially by herring gulls, which wait for parent birds to return from fishing trips and then rob them of their catch. The ever-present gulls wait to grab puffin chicks, too, as the little ones cry for food and peek from their underground nest burrows.

Puffins usually mate for life. They may spend months apart, but they recognize their mate when they return to their island home. During courtship, the male and female vigorously rub beaks, frequently opening their brightly colored bills to display the brilliant orange mouth lining. This activity appears to be very interesting to other puffins which crowd in so close that they almost fall on top of the loving birds.

Even when the male puffin is following the female in the water, they are often surrounded by other puffins. Sometimes a ring of puffins circles a mating pair. The spectators push each other, turning their heads back and forth until all the birds are too close together. The certain distance that must be maintained between each bird is broken; the birds must regroup. Suddenly all the watchers dive together under

A pair of puffins vigorously engages in a billing bout, while an interested neighbor watches.

the water. But the chase of the loving birds often continues. Their mating takes place on the water.

Both the female and the male puffin share in the digging of the nest, which is a tunnel that can be as long as eight feet. They use their heavy bills as pickaxes and their clawed, webbed feet as shovels. Both birds carry grass deep into the nesting cavity. There one egg is laid.

The two birds continue to work together, often rubbing beaks. Before one bird takes its turn sitting on the egg it may rub its beak on its mate's. The puffins incubate their egg—both day and night—for about forty-two days. Once the black downy chick hatches, both parents tirelessly feed it for about six weeks.

To humans who cannot fully understand the communications between birds, puffins appear to do some very funny things. Sometimes they even seem to play. People have seen two puffins having a "tug-of-war" with a piece of grass, pulling each other back and forth so hard that each bird topples forward in turn.

The curious puffins peck at anything of interest—their neighbor's metal leg band or the red rim of its eye.

Puffins sometimes parade around carrying loads of grass as big as their heads. Grass and gull feathers are taken into burrows to help build a nest at the back of their earthen tunnel.

Puffins are usually quiet birds, but sometimes they do make

A pair of puffins stands outside their rock burrow at Machias Seal Island. The mouth open gape is a social greeting between mated pairs.

interesting sounds. They purr and croak during pretend fights. One of their calls sounds very much like a loud chain saw.

The Latin name for the puffin is *Fratercula arctica*, which means "Little Brother of the Arctic." Perhaps this name shows how people feel about this sturdy little bird. They feel a brotherhood of spirit.

3. DANGERS IN THE PAST

Puffins seem curious and unafraid of people, sometimes flying or paddling as close as ten feet to make an inspection. The birds will circle boats, flying away and then returning for a closer look. This trusting attitude has meant danger for the puffin and its relatives.

One hundred and fifty years ago, the puffin had a distant relative called the great auk. This flightless bird stood thirty inches tall. It was not aggressive and was even more helpless than the puffin.

People hunted auks for feathers and for meat. They exterminated them, not leaving any breeding pairs. Whole colonies of these birds disappeared. Using clubs, sailors could slay enough auks in just thirty minutes to fill two big open boats. One Englishman captured hundreds of live auks by spreading a canvas sail from the shore to his anchored ship.

He filled the hold of his boat by simply marching the birds across the sail.

Natural disasters also affected the auk. One entire breeding island sank into the sea because of a volcanic explosion. Finally, in 1844, someone killed an auk to take its body to a museum. It was the last of the species. Never again would there be such a bird on earth.

About one hundred years ago puffins were hunted in this country. People ate puffin flesh and used it for fishing bait.

People also hunted puffins because they wanted their feathers to stuff pillows and mattresses. Entire wings decorated ladies' hats. A hunter might be paid forty cents for one wing—a lot of money at that time. Thousands of birds died for "fashion."

People caught the gentle seabirds by spreading fishing nets over nesting burrows at night. In the morning, puffin parents were trapped by the nets when they came out of their burrows. Little chicks, coming out at night, were hopelessly entangled, too.

In a single day one hunter could capture almost one hundred puffins. All day long the screams of dying seabirds could be heard above the sounds of the crashing waves and the howling wind.

No thought was given to the future of the bird colonies.

Puffins at Matinicus Rock, a U.S. Coast Guard Light Station.

People dug up burrows to find eggs and baby chicks. By 1906 the five Maine islands that had been covered with thousands of busy puffins in 1810 were almost empty of life. Only one pair of puffins was reported on Matinicus Rock.

Even now, after years of protection by the wardens who run the lighthouse on Matinicus Rock, there are less than one hundred breeding pairs of Atlantic puffins on this last and only breeding island remaining in the United States. "Little Brother of the Arctic" is in danger. He, too, could disappear forever from the earth.

4. NATURAL DANGERS

Like the auk, the puffin faces natural disasters. One danger comes from the way in which these birds live so closely together. Because their burrows are often interconnected and crowded near one another in loose soil, the roofs and the walls of the tunnels become weak as the burrows are enlarged. Sometimes the nest areas collapse.

Then, the baby birds push out of their broken homes, exposing themselves to damp, cold weather. Unable to warm themselves, they sicken and die. Other puffin babies die when ever-watchful gulls, sitting on the tops of their burrows, snatch them up.

The gulls are a constant danger even when the burrows are sturdy. They rob parent birds of fish as the puffins return to their burrows. Hungry chicks may wander out of their tunnels only to become additional gull food.

Flying herring gull, a puffin predator whose numbers have greatly increased.

Mammals pose a threat, too. Brown rats, weasels, and raccoons can crawl into burrows and eat puffin chicks. One busy colony, crowded with thousands of burrows containing baby birds, can be destroyed quickly by a few of these animals. This happened in 1817 when a ship was wrecked off the coast of England. The rats from the boat swam ashore and ate every baby puffin they could find. Only the few chicks which lived in burrows on steep cliffs escaped. Now rats, not puffins, occupy the island.

Even tiny spider-like animals called ticks can bother puffin chicks. They cause infections in the chicks' eyes and ears, and then the little ones can become weak, sick, and often die.

Enemies lurk in the water, too. While young puffins are potential food for the gulls that come from the sky, puffins of all ages are in danger from larger fish.

5. DANGERS FROM HUMANS

People can be enemies of the puffin, too.

Even people who like the puffin may be dangerous to its survival. Bird watchers and photographers sometimes come too near to nesting sites. Low-flying planes can upset parent birds by buzzing their nesting areas. The frightened creatures flutter about excitedly.

In Iceland, where puffins are very abundant, people still hunt the puffin and eat its meat. In the North Atlantic Ocean fishermen catch the food of the puffin. Modern fishing boats spread huge nets over miles of ocean, taking billions of small and large fish. The Portuguese and the Russians are fishing extensively for a small fish called capelin. This fish is the puffins' main food source. If too many capelin are caught, thousands of puffins may starve . . . especially those that nest or swim near fishing grounds.

Puffin returning to its burrow with a fish intended for its single youngster. Puffins can feed up to 100 miles from their nesting island.

Modern life-style exposes the puffin to other dangers as well. When chemicals are sprayed on plants, they are washed downhill by rain, running into streams and rivers, and finally spilling into the ocean. Then the poison enters the tiny plants and animals that live in the ocean water. Fish eat these plants and animals. When the puffin eats these fish, the poison enters the body of the puffin.

Some birds which have eaten such chemicals lay eggs with very thin, weak shells. These eggs break. The baby birds never hatch, and the bird population decreases. This problem may be a factor in the decline of the razorbill—a bird that is a close relative of the puffin.

Oil spills are another very serious danger to the puffins. Minor spills occur during the normal deep-sea drilling process. Large amounts of oil spill out when rigs are not working correctly, or when tanks are routinely cleaned at sea. Huge oil spills occur when tankers have accidents at sea.

Then, extensive, black pools of oil float on the ocean surface. Because the puffin is a diving bird, it is more apt to dive into the sticky tar than to fly away. All fall, winter, and early spring the puffins swim on the open ocean, covering thousands of miles. Therefore, the puffin is more likely to

Puffins raft in the sea near their nesting islands.

run into oil spills than other birds. Even one small spot of oil on its feathers spells disaster. As it preens with its bill and wipes its head over its feathers, it spreads this oil over its body. Its own perfect waterproofing is destroyed; the icy water then leaks through the outer protective feathers and chills its body—causing the puffin to freeze and die.

Even now, oil is being pumped from offshore oil rigs near Witless Bay, Newfoundland. One huge oil spill could mean a quick end for most of the Atlantic puffins left in North America, since almost three-fourths of the population breed in this area. And oil drilling is planned for Georges Banks off the coast of the United States, where currents and storms could carry the deadly tar into the remaining areas where puffins live.

Even though there are still thousands of puffins, there are only a few breeding colonies. It would be easy for them to disappear. Too many gulls, predatory mammals, insufficient food, eggs that do not hatch, or oil slicks could cause thousands of puffins to die within a few years since these birds usually return to the same breeding area *even if something is wrong.*

6. SAVING THE PUFFIN

But just as there are people who do not care about the birds and animals of the world, there are also people who care very much. These people love the beauty and variety that different kinds of plants and animals add to human life. Many of these people also understand that birds and animals act as "early warning systems" for people. Because humans, animals, and plants are all living things, they are often affected by the same problems. When a species begins to disappear, the reasons for its disappearance may also be affecting humans.

In the 1800s, coal miners knew about early warning systems. They took canaries down into the mines. If the canaries became sick and died, the miners knew that invisible, poisonous gases were spreading through the underground tunnels. The smaller, more sensitive bodies of the birds responded quickly to the poisons. The men would hurry away from the

Stephen Kress placing a puffin chick in its new burrow at Eastern Egg Rock at night, after its one hundred mile trip from Great Island, Newfoundland.

deadly tunnels into the safer air. The canaries had helped to save their lives.

Some people care very deeply about the survival of the "Little Brother of the Arctic." One of them is Dr. Stephen Kress, an ornithologist with the National Audubon Society. Steve has always loved animals . . . frogs, snakes, and crippled birds of prey. He loved the state of Maine—its plants, its birdlife, and especially the puffins. During the summers that he worked in Maine, he learned about the puffins' habits and grew to admire the bird.

As he grew up, he determined that he wanted to bring back some of the beauty that had disappeared from our earth. "I felt that we had lost something special. I imagined the puffins as they had once been—standing atop Eastern Egg Rock, an island I had come to know as an ornithology instructor at the nearby Audubon Camp in Maine. This vision haunted me as I read everything available about puffins and pursued the idea of reestablishing a puffin colony with anyone whom I thought might offer help."

Steve realized that it might be possible to reestablish the puffins because of three important facts: these birds do not need the warmth of their parents after they are one week old; they are never seen with their parents after leaving the nest; and they usually return to breed in the same place where they hatched.

Somehow puffins remember their hatching place. The

process is called "imprinting." Steve thought, "If very young puffins could be brought to an island in Maine and raised there successfully, perhaps a new breeding colony could be established." Steve also felt that if he were successful, other people might try to start new colonies of puffins or other seabirds at former breeding areas. Never before had such an experiment been attempted!

7. BEGINNING
THE EXPERIMENT

So in 1973, helped by the National Audubon Society and the Canadian Wildlife Service, and by other people who believed in the project, Steve and several researchers began their "re-establishment" project. They flew to Newfoundland and took a boat to Great Island. As they walked to the burrows to collect baby puffin chicks, hundreds of thousands of seabirds circled and screamed overhead. Razorbills, guillemots, murres, gulls, and terns shared the world of the puffin.

Great care had to be taken not to fall through the soil into the holes that had been burrowed by the puffins. Carefully, the ornithologists walked along the steep slopes and reached into the burrows, looking for two-week-old chicks. They were only permitted to take six chicks until they had proven to the Canadian Wildlife Service that they could raise

Collecting puffin chicks at Great Island, Newfoundland.

healthy birds. By measuring the length of the wings, they could tell the age of the baby puffins.

Some of the burrows were empty; others contained biting parent birds. The burrows always ended in a sharp turn that opened into a nesting area. Some of the burrow tunnels were longer than the researchers' arms so they could not reach those chicks.

Finally, six healthy young chicks were found and brought back to the Audubon Camp laboratory on Hog Island in

Maine. One puffin baby did not live; a raccoon found the burrow in which it was being raised and ate it. Up until that time no raccoon had ever been reported on Hog Island!

When the remaining five chicks were about six week old, they were old enough to leave their burrows. Bands were attached to their legs. Each chick wore a green plastic band on its left leg and a metal band on its right leg. The chicks were placed into special, artificial burrows constructed in rock crevices on a nearby island in Muscongus Bay, called Eastern Egg Rock, once the site of a thriving puffin colony.

Throughout the entire experiment Steve and his researchers kept detailed notes on the puffins' activities. The descrip-

The first five puffin chicks peer from their transport box after arrival at Eastern Egg Rock for release in 1973.

Aerial view of Eastern Egg Rock Island.

tion at the departure of the chicks in 1973 follows: "During the first night on Eastern Egg Rock all of the young emerged from their burrows several times to exercise their wings. Two of the young birds walked down to the slope from the burrows and swam off to sea. The remaining three birds returned to their burrows until the following night. On the night of August 19th all three birds again emerged to exercise their wings. Two birds then walked to the sea edge and swam away. The third climbed atop a rock and flew out to sea."

No green-banded birds have ever returned to Eastern Egg Rock. Perhaps none survived, since many young birds die at sea. Steve continued the experiment, though, bringing back more chicks the following spring.

8. GROWING UP ON EASTERN EGG ROCK

In 1974, the ornithologists reached into hundreds of burrows. They captured fifty-four baby puffins and put them into carrying cases, constructed out of twelve-ounce orange juice cans. To keep the ten-day-old chicks from slipping and to help them stay clean, sand grains were glued to the bottom of each can. To also help keep the birds clean, the amount of droppings were reduced by not feeding the chicks during the trip from Newfoundland to Maine. Each case was covered with burlap so that the chicks could breathe but would not see their surroundings. Most of the chicks were silent in the cases except for an occasional high-pitched whine. Finally, after travelling one thousand miles and fourteen hours by car, boat, truck, and plane, and after being examined by veterinarians, the young birds were brought directly to their new Maine home—Eastern Egg Rock Island.

Puffin chicks in carrying case.

This small, treeless, flat island is located eight miles out to sea from the Audubon summer camp on Hog Island. No mammals live on Eastern Egg Rock, and the soil in the center of the island is soft. During the early spring months of 1974, Steve and his assistants had built burrows for the baby puffins.

After arrival, each small black chick was gently placed in its own burrow. Every bird disappeared quickly inside its new home. Small fish were left at the entrance of each hole; during the first week wire doors were placed over the burrow entrances to prevent hungry gulls from snatching the puffin babies.

A puffin chick, 10 days old, at time of transplant from New-foundland.

9. PREPARING THE NESTING SITE

The researchers had to do the work of the parent birds. Each precious baby had to be kept safe and healthy. Only with dedicated care would the young birds survive.

The gulls which lived and nested on Eastern Egg Rock were a problem to the ornithologists. Open garbage dumps and fish canning factories on the mainland provided the gulls with plenty of food. Thus, there were more gulls than there had ever been before.

To prepare Eastern Egg Rock for the puffin-raising experiment, biologists from the U.S. Fish and Wildlife Service had smashed gull eggs and spread poisoned bread around to reduce the large gull population. At Eastern Egg Rock, only gulls eat bread; most other seabirds eat fish. When the gulls learned to tell poisoned bread from other bread, the government agents returned to shoot some of the gulls. Killing gulls

52

Ceramic puffin burrow, an experimental design in 1974.

was difficult for these bird-loving people to do, but there was no choice.

It was difficult for humans to construct safe, dry burrows for puffin chicks. Most of the first burrows were made out of tiles with earth and grass placed on top of them. The researchers tried to make homes that looked like rock crevices. Tiles were easy to get and work with. The fronts of the burrows were covered with hinged wooden doors that contained openings for the chicks.

Some of the little puffins suffered in these homes. The

temperature in the burrows was too high; more soil was put on top of the tiles. Some of the burrows were too damp because water flooded into them or because water condensed on the tile walls. Double layers of netting were put on wooden frames in the backs of the burrows to keep the chicks from touching the wet walls.

The tile burrows also became dirty because the chicks were going to the bathroom in their nest chambers. Dirty burrows soiled the birds' feathers which must stay clean in order to be waterproof at fledging time. Lice and ticks were found on a few chicks. The researchers had to open the burrow doors and sweep the nest areas clean with a spoon. The ticks were carefully removed with tweezers and the lice dusted with a special powder. The work was tedious and time consuming.

Because the researchers were learning about raising puffin chicks, they tried different ways to solve these problems. First, they put rocks in some of the burrows for the babies to sit on so they had a clean place on which to rest. The human helpers decreased the size of the burrow openings so less light came into the tunnels. As the baby puffins became older they felt safer, and kept going farther out into the entrance tunnel to go to the bathroom, or "squirt." Because the workers wanted the baby puffins to be a little overweight, they had fed them more food than the babies would have received from their parents "in the wild." When the workers fed them less, the amount of their droppings decreased.

Puffin burrows under construction at Eastern Egg Rock. Ground floor shows L shape. When complete, they will have a sod roof.

Each year the puffin-raising experiment continued, and the researchers learned more about taking care of the baby birds. Later burrows were kept cleaner because they were constructed from sod (soil and grass). The puffin chicks, as they enlarged their little homes, kicked the loose soil around inside their nest chambers, burying their droppings.

10. RAISING YOUNG PUFFINS

Feeding as many as one hundred baby puffins was a daily challenge for the·workers. In the beginning they fed each chick three times a day. Smelts were fed to the chicks because they are similar to the capelin fish on which the puffins are usually fed. One puffin chick eats about two hundred fish during its four weeks at Eastern Egg Rock. Each smelt had to be defrosted and rinsed with seawater so that it would be easy to swallow. Then the fish was cut in half so that the puffin would not choke.

Three times a week something special was put into the mouths of some of the smelts. It was one of three different vitamin pills. Steve felt that the chicks would need all the strength they could get and the freezing process destroyed certain important vitamins in the smelts.

Sometimes there were feeding problems. In 1975, the

Placing a vitamin capsule in frozen smelt intended for trans-planted young puffin.

pieces of fish were getting too dirty because of the loose soil around the burrow entrances. The researchers realized that had the puffins' parents been there, they would have packed down the soil. So they wet it themselves and packed it down!

The researchers were also concerned that the puffin chicks might see too much of their human "parents." They were worried that this association might affect their behavior.

Assistant Tom Fleischner placing meal of thawed smelt at the mouth of an artificial sod burrow.

Thus, the number of daily feedings was reduced to two. The smelts were carefully placed at the entrances of the burrows, so that the birds would not get too familiar with human hands.

Sometimes the observers were fooled by the behavior of the baby chicks when they tried to record what was happening to each chick. Once, Chick Number One went into Chick Number Seven's burrow. Then the researchers had to find the missing puffin, otherwise the two babies would not get enough food. At other times some of the chicks would wander into empty burrows. The researchers stopped this practice by blocking the entrances of those burrows with rocks.

When the chicks were about three weeks old they became more active and began to "squirt" just outside their burrows. They also went outside their burrows at night to exercise their wings. Perhaps it was at these times that they learned that Eastern Egg Rock was their home.

Because the researchers wanted to find out as much as they could about the behavior of the birds, they put two drinking straws across each entrance hole. If the straws were knocked down during the night, the workers knew that the birds had come out. They wanted to know more. By spreading sand in front of the burrow entrances, they could tell in the morning what the puffins had been doing during the night. If the sand had been moved around, the birds were stretching and exercising, not just "squirting."

11. CHICK PERSONALITIES

Each summer Steve and the men and women with whom he worked learned more about the personalities of the puffins. In 1976, a special "blind" was built over four puffin burrows. The top of each burrow was covered with clear Plexiglas. The dark blind was lighted only by an infrared light, so as not to disturb the puffins. By watching the chicks' daily activities, the researchers learned some surprising facts.

The chicks were very busy in their nest chambers. Some of the baby birds carried grass in their bills and moved it around their nest area. Most of the puffins spent a lot of time exercising, opening their wings slowly over and over again, or folding them, or beating them up and down vigorously. Other exercises included wing-leg stretching, head scratching, and head shaking. They also exercised by digging, thus

A five-week-old puffin can consume six pieces of fish in ten seconds, as viewed in this underground scene in its Egg Rock burrow.

enlarging their burrows and making more room in which to exercise.

Baby chicks pecked a lot . . . at the floor, at pieces of grass, at roots growing inside their tunnels, and at living things like snails and insects. Some of the young birds seemed afraid of insects and ran into their nests when a fly buzzed by. Others grabbed flies and pecked at mosquitoes.

The chicks definitely had different personalities. Some birds disappeared into the nests at feeding time. Later they returned to eat. Others ate as soon as the smelts were put in their burrows. A few aggressive babies even lunged at the worker's hand, biting at fingers.

Some of the young puffins spent most of their time in the darkest, farthest part of their burrows, while others moved closer to the entrance as they grew older. Some of the chicks liked the night life so well that they often came out of their burrows. While some of the birds were messy, others were neat . . . carefully "squirting" on the outside wall of their burrow entrances.

Some of the babies were quiet birds; others always waited excitedly for their food. In 1976, Number Seventy-seven peeked out from his hole and called louder than any other baby.

12. THE WORK
OF A RESEARCHER

Each summer the three people who came to live on Eastern Egg Rock worked hard. Two researchers at a time stayed on the small island. They worked and rested in a small tent. A flag with a puffin drawn on it flew outside. Every day the baby birds were fed two or three times. Each feeding took at least an hour. Every four days some of the babies were weighed, measured, and photographed. Weakened burrows were rebuilt. The researchers were quiet while they worked with the birds so that there would be as little contact with human voices as possible. Records were meticulously kept on the puffins' activities and progress, as well as on other birds and plant life on Eastern Egg Rock. The researchers worked to protect the Arctic terns and the storm petrels. The aggressive terns will fight gulls; therefore, their presence acts as a "safety umbrella" for the puffin colony. Special plants, eliminated

Research assistant Bob Wesley photographs a puffin chick as part of a detailed study of plumage growth.

Tent site at Eastern Egg Rock, with project flag and weather equipment visible.

long ago by grazing sheep, were transplanted to Eastern Egg Rock. The Audubon people wanted to give the plants—like the puffins—a safe place to live.

Weather conditions were recorded. Research work also included the banding of puffin chicks and other birds. Each year a different colored band was attached to the leg of each young puffin. The number on the band matched the number of the burrow in which the chick had been raised. By observing the number printed on the band, researchers in future years could know which birds were returning to Eastern Egg Rock.

Sometimes the work was lonely and boring. At times it was also annoying and dangerous. The wind blew persistently, sometimes pushing rainwater right through the tent material. The flag pole blew over. Water crashed on rocks and made spouts that rose forty feet above Eastern Egg Rock. Everything was covered with salt spray. At times the tent leaked. Every piece of clothing and bedding became soaked!

During rough weather, boats could not land with food

Banding a puffin chick at Eastern Egg Rock. Stephen Kress, right, with two research assistants, Evelyn Weinstein and Tom Fleischner.

Color leg bands and metal U.S. Fish and Wildlife Service bands will help researchers recognize transplanted puffins when they are sighted.

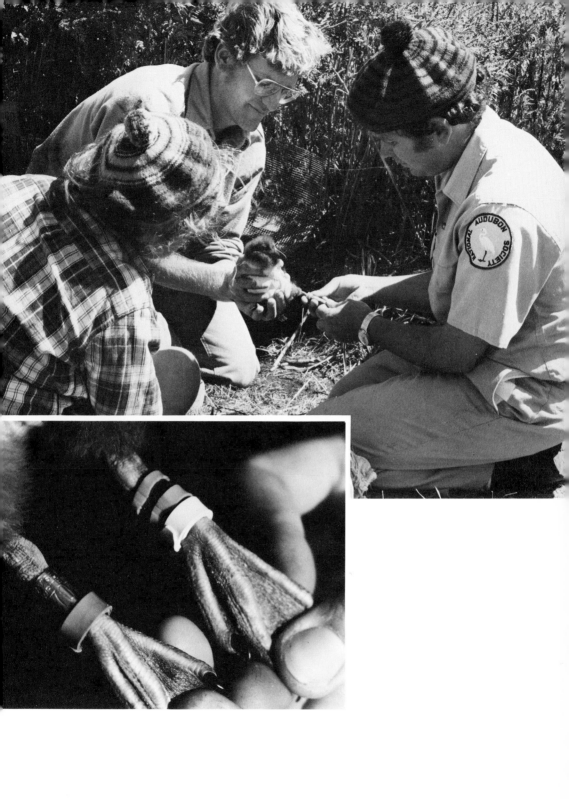

Stephen W. Kress with a six-week-old puffin chick at Eastern Egg Rock.

or with the third relief researcher. At other times the assistants could not leave the island. Sometimes waves overturned their boat, and they cut their hands on rough barnacles as they struggled to upright it. During calmer weather ragweed pollen and stinging nettles annoyed the workers. August mosquitoes sent them into their tents at sundown.

In spite of these problems, however, the weeks on Eastern Egg Rock were mostly beautiful and exciting. In 1978, 139 different kinds of birds came to visit the small area. One day in May twenty-five thousand ducks passed through. In fact, Eastern Egg Rock is such an important seabird nesting site that it was leased to the National Audubon Society by the Maine Bureau of Public Lands. In 1976 Eastern Egg Rock was named the Allan D. Cruickshank Audubon Wildlife Sanctuary. Now black guillemots, Leach's storm petrels, eider ducks, and puffins are protected there.

Fifty-eight different kinds of plants grow on the tiny, rocky island. Blossoms seem almost to burst forth from rocky crevices. Arctic terns circle over yellow warblers. Great blue herons stand quietly in pools of water, while baleen whales surface in the hazy distance. Harbor seals grunt on the rocks; gray storm petrels purr in the night air. At times the great Northern Lights fill the dark sky with their special eerie green radiance. Then the researchers know that they are seeing sights and hearing sounds that very few people ever experience.

13. THE FLEDGLING

Each summer the most exciting experience was the dramatic exit of the young puffin, or "fledgling" as it is called at this stage of its six-week-old life. For several weeks the young bird has been busy exercising both inside the burrow during the day and outside at night, the time when it is safe from predators. The fledgling eats little food or none at all during the final days in the burrow. Puffins reared by their own parents show the same behavior.

Then, one night in August while the gulls are asleep, one young puffin may go far from its burrow for the first time, walking downhill to the sea. A few others may also leave. The metal bands on their legs hit the rocks. "Clink! Clink! Clink!" The researchers can hear them leaving. Sometimes the puffins leave on moonlit nights, their white breasts glowing, but they also leave even in dark, stormy weather.

A puffin fledgling at about six weeks of age exercises its wings outside its new home. Bands identify it as a transplanted bird.

When the fledglings reach the edge of the boulders, they jump, fly, or hurl themselves toward the black water below. Each night more young birds fledge, and by the end of August all the burrows are empty. They have never flown before, never swum before, or fished for their food before. They are alone at sea. They must feed and protect themselves. It is not surprising that many baby puffins do not survive the first months of their difficult independent lives.

73

The researchers have completed their work. In some ways the young birds have received better care than they would have received in the wild.

From 1973 through 1980, 630 baby puffins were raised at Eastern Egg Rock. During this period only twenty-seven baby birds died, far fewer than would have died under natural conditions.

Once the puffins have left their burrow homes, the test of life survival begins. For at least two years these young birds swim in the vast Atlantic Ocean, hunting fish, resting, floating, weathering storms until, in the spring of their second or third year, some instinct will hopefully bring them back to their home island, Eastern Egg Rock.

Although the first reestablished puffins left in 1973, no puffins returned to Eastern Egg Rock in 1974, in 1975, or even in 1976. In 1976, the 1974 babies would have been two years old and perhaps ready to return. It was difficult for the ornithologists not to become discouraged . . . so many people had worked so hard and given so much time and money to the experiment.

Young puffins spend at least the first two years of life at sea without coming to land. Adults spend eight months of each year at sea.

14. COME BACK, LITTLE BROTHER

Then Steve had an idea. He knew that young puffins would be most attracted to the island if older birds were also there. Since there were no adult puffins breeding and raising chicks on Eastern Egg Rock, Steve decided to use wooden carvings or decoys to attract live puffins. He hoped the puffins would land to inspect the wooden birds, thereby becoming more familiar with Eastern Egg Rock—the island on which they had been raised.

Using a stuffed bird as a guide, an expert wood-carver created two models—a standing puffin and a swimming puffin. These birds were then reproduced on a carving machine. The rotating knives cut out forty-eight standing and forty-eight swimming birds. Each bird was carefully painted and sealed by volunteers at the Cornell Laboratory of Ornithology.

Research assistant Kathy Blanchard painting puffin decoys.

Then, the floating decoys were attached to anchor lines with leather thongs. The standing birds had metal rods extending downward from their bellies which were inserted into bases in the boulders of Eastern Egg Rock. By May, 1977, nearly one hundred adult puffin decoys were grouped around Eastern Egg Rock in lifelike positions.

The decoys looked very real and fooled many living creatures. Black-backed gulls swooped down and knocked the models over with their feet. After a short time the big birds realized that the wooden puffins were not behaving normally; they left the decoys alone and even sat among them as if they were rocks.

The floating decoys also fooled many people who had come to take pictures of puffins. One lady took a wonderful photograph of one puffin on the water. When she developed the photograph, however, she discovered it was just a black-and-white decoy!

15. FRATERCULA ARCTICA

Then, on June 12, 1977, something wonderful happened. A live, adult puffin landed on Eastern Egg Rock near one of the decoys. There was a white band on his leg, showing that he was one of the young birds which had fledged from Eastern Egg Rock in 1975. Now he was two years old. Somehow he had survived the beaks of gulls, the jaws of big fish, oil spills, storms, and all the dangers that must be faced during two winters on the open ocean. He had learned to feed himself, and he had found his way back to the island on which he had been raised, but not born. Part of Steve Kress's experiment had worked. Even though this bird had been born in New-foundland, he had grown up near the Maine coast. The location of Eastern Egg Rock had been imprinted successfully on his brain. This was his real home, and he had come back, this Little Brother of the Arctic.

A banded puffin has returned to Eastern Egg Rock and finds company among a wooden decoy welcoming committee.

Banded puffin investigating wooden decoys at Eastern Egg Rock.

During that summer of 1977, and the following two summers, the researchers saw more puffins; many of them wore the colored bands. The puffins were often attracted to the standing decoys, bowing low to them or pecking at their tails and bellies. Some of the live puffins even seem attracted to the decoys and rubbed their bills up and down the beaks of the wooden birds. Then, after taking a closer look and receiving no response, they walked away.

However, in 1977, these returning adults did not seem interested in the floating decoys, although one puffin did seem to like a red-and-white lobster pot buoy. As it bobbed up and down in the water, the puffin pushed against it, swam around his new "toy," pecking and nibbling at it.

Because puffins like to be with other puffins—especially during the summer months—Steve created another puffin attraction. A box with mirrors on all four sides was placed on

A young puffin investigates a bright red and white lobster trap buoy in the water off Eastern Egg Rock.

Puffins investigate their reflections in a four-sided mirror box.

A banded puffin explores a rock crevice at Eastern Egg Rock.

top of one of the boulders on Eastern Egg Rock. Lone puffins would then see their moving reflections. As they walked around the box, new puffins seemed to come into view. The box was a source of great interest. Even groups of puffins stared, pecked, and pushed at it.

During the summer of 1980, there were 896 puffin sightings at Eastern Egg Rock. As many as twenty-three puffins were seen at the same time, standing on rocks and exploring under the huge boulders. Some birds were also observed rubbing bills. In the year or two before puffins reach breeding age, this increased social activity is common behavior. A few of the birds were unbanded, perhaps having come from other colonies. Banded birds from Eastern Egg Rock were also seen on the other islands. Some of the puffins were sighted on Matinicus Rock, the closest breeding colony, and on Machias Seal Island, a breeding colony in Canada that is 125 miles away.

None of the puffins bred, however, since they usually do not breed until they are least five years old. In 1981 the white-banded birds, born in 1975, will be over six years old. No one is sure what will happen then—and during the years that follow.

16. AN UNKNOWN FUTURE

Steve Kress's experiment is not finished. There are still many unanswered questions. Are males more likely to return than females? At what age will they breed? Will enough of the Eastern Egg Rock puffins survive to breeding maturity? How many puffins are necessary to begin a colony and then to keep it going? Will the puffins even begin a new breeding colony at Eastern Egg Rock if there are no older adult birds there? Puffins wearing Eastern Egg Rock bands have been seen on Matinicus Rock, twenty-six miles away. Will the birds raised on Eastern Egg Rock choose to breed at nearby Matinicus Rock where other adult puffins are already breeding? In the summer of 1980, one transplanted puffin did raise a chick on Matinicus Rock. This is the first known transplanted puffin to breed away from its birth place. When Matinicus Rock becomes crowded, will the transplanted puffins begin

A banded puffin stands with an un-banded puffin at Matinicus Rock.

breeding at Eastern Egg Rock? If the birds do remain at Eastern Egg Rock, will they choose sod burrows like the ones in which they were raised or will they choose to nest under boulders as the original breeding puffins did? Have the unbanded puffins that have come to Eastern Egg Rock lost their bands or have they come from other colonies? Where do puffins go after leaving Eastern Egg Rock? How long do puffins live?

If Steve Kress's experiment works, other puffin colonies may be started in other areas of the North Atlantic. More colonies will mean more chances for the survival of *Fratercula arctica*.

If Steve Kress' experiment works, other puffin colonies birds have a greater hope of succeeding because of the knowledge gained from this important first experiment. Efforts to revive a lost Arctic tern colony have already begun.

Perhaps we will, as Steve Kress says, ". . . be able to right some of the wrongs that earlier people have done to our environment."

INDEX

Aggressiveness, puffins and, 22–23, 63

Allan D. Cruickshank Audubon Wildlife Sanctuary, 71

Appearance. *See* Puffins

Auks, great, 29–30, 33

Beak (bill). *See* Puffins

Blanchard, Kathy, 77

Burrows, 25, 33, 37, 45, 46, 47, 48, 49, 50, 60, 61, 63, 72, 73, 90
  ceramic, 53–54
  sod, 55

Canada, 19, 86

Canadian Wildlife Service, 45

Canaries, coal miners and, 41, 43

Capelin, 37

Care of young, 25, 52, 75

Cheeks. *See* Puffins

Chemicals, danger to puffins, 38

Cornell Laboratory of Ornithology, 76

Courtship, 23, 25

Dangers faced by puffins, 29–40, 79

Decoys, puffin, 76–78, 79–83

Disasters, natural, 33–36

Ducks, 71

Ears. *See* Puffins

Eastern Egg Rock Island, 42, 43, 47, 48–90

Eggs, puffin, 25, 38

Eyes. *See* Puffins

Face. *See* Puffins

Feathers. *See* Puffins

Feet. *See* Puffins

Females, 19, 23, 25, 87

Fighting, puffins and, 23, 24, 28

Fledglings, 72–75

Fleischner, Tom, 58, 69

Food, 37, 56–60, 62, 72, 73

Fratercula arctica, 28, 90

Future, puffins and the, 87, 90

Great Island, Newfoundland, 15, 16–17, 45, 46

Greenland, 19
Guillemots, 45, 71
Gulls, 23, 33, 34–35, 40, 45, 50,
    52, 64, 72, 78, 79

Hatching, 43
Herons, 71
Hog Island, 46, 47, 50
Horned puffins, 19

Iceland, 19, 37
Imprinting, 44, 79

Kress, Stephen, 42, 43–44, 45, 47,
    48, 50, 56, 61, 69, 70, 76, 79,
    83, 87, 90

Leg bands, 25, 47, 68, 69, 72, 79,
    82, 86, 87, 90
Legs. See Puffins
Lice, 54
"Little Brother of the Arctic," 28,
    43

Machias Seal Island, 26–27, 86
Males, 19, 22, 23, 25, 87
Mating, 23, 25
Matinicus Rock, 15, 18, 31, 32, 86,
    87, 88
Murres, 45
Muscongus Bay, 47

National Audubon Society, 45, 68,
    71
Nests. See Burrows
Northern Lights, 71

Oil spills, 39–40

Pecking, 23, 25, 63, 82, 83, 86

People, as danger to puffins, 29–32,
    37–40
Personalities of puffins, 61–63
Petrels, storm, 64, 71
Playing, 25
Predators, 23, 33, 34–35, 36, 72
Puffins
    appearance, 13, 20, 22
    beak (bill), 21, 22, 23, 24, 25,
        40, 61, 82, 86
    cheeks, 20
    ears, 36
    eyes, 14–15, 20, 22, 25, 36
    face, 22
    feathers, 13, 20, 23, 30, 40, 54
    feet, 13, 22, 25
    legs, 22
    wings, 13, 14, 30, 46, 48, 60,
        61, 73

Raccoons, 36, 47
Rats, 36
Razorbills, 39, 45

Scotland, 19
Seals, 71
Smelts, 56, 57, 58, 63
Sounds, 28, 49, 63

Terns, 45, 64, 71, 90
Ticks, 36, 54
Tufted puffins, 19

Vitamins, 56, 57

Warblers, 71
Weasels, 36
Weinstein, Evelyn, 68
Whales, 71
Wings. See Puffins